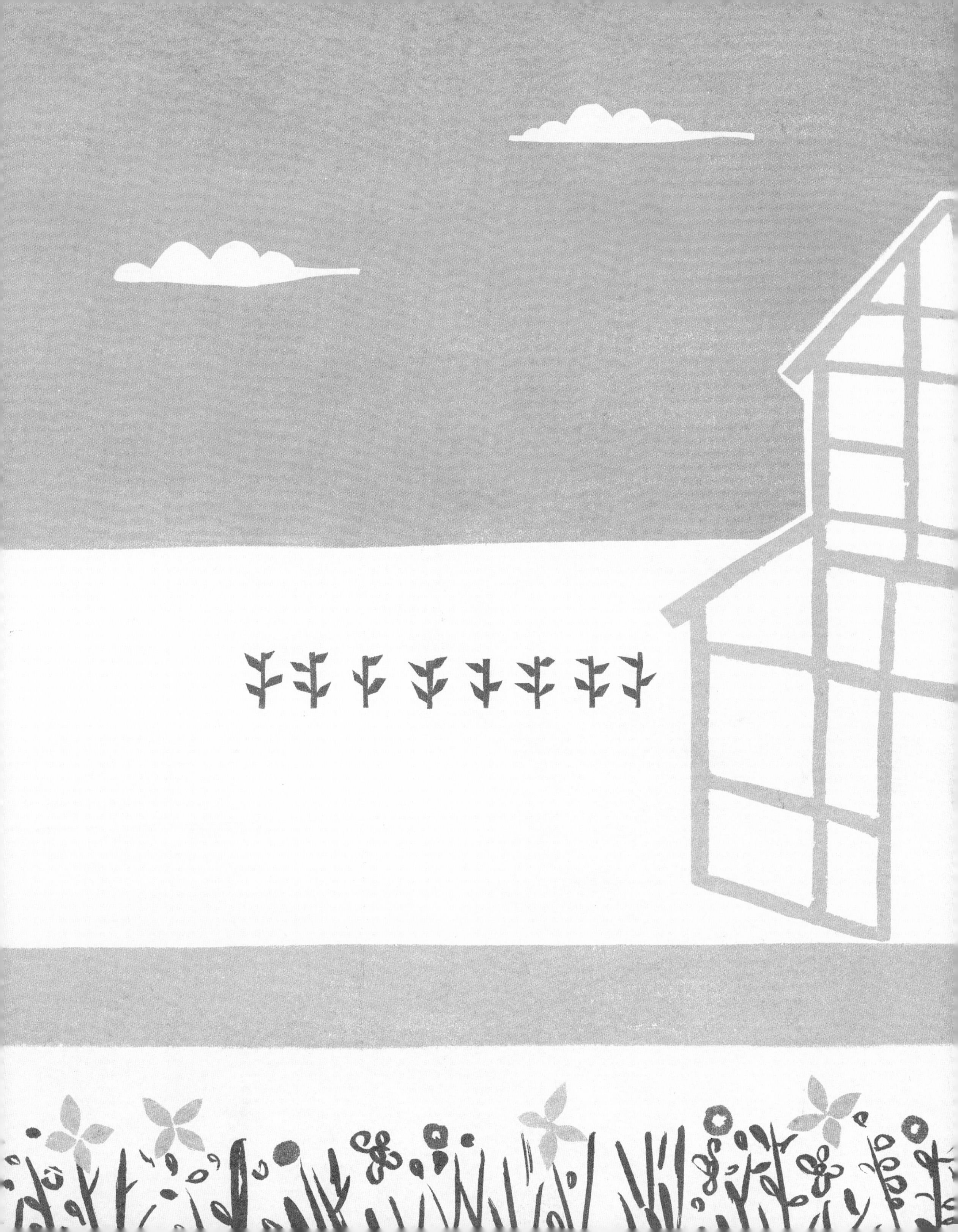

For Carrie

—Jarrett

For Marcela

—Jerome

For information about permission to reproduce selections from this book, write to Permissions,
W. W. Norton & Company, Inc., 500 Fifth Avenue, New York, NY 10110

For information about special discounts for bulk purchases, please contact
W. W. Norton Special Sales at specialsales@wwnorton.com or 800-233-4830

Library of Congress Cataloging-in-Publication Data

Names: Pumphrey, Jarrett, author. | Pumphrey, Jerome, author.
Title: The old truck / Jarrett Pumphrey, Jerome Pumphrey.
Description: New York : Norton Young Readers, an imprint of W. W. Norton and Company, [2020] | Audience: Ages 3-5.
Identifiers: LCCN 2019027692 | ISBN 9781324005193 (hardcover) | ISBN 9781324005209 (epub)
Subjects: CYAC: Trucks—Fiction. | Farm life—Fiction. | African Americans—Fiction.
Classification: LCC PZ7.P97328 Old 2020 | DDC [E]—dc23
LC record available at https://lccn.loc.gov/2019027692

W. W. Norton & Company, Inc., 500 Fifth Avenue, New York, N.Y. 10110
www.wwnorton.com

W. W. Norton & Company Ltd., 15 Carlisle Street, London W1D 3BS

5 6 7 8 9 0

Jarrett Pumphrey   Jerome Pumphrey

THE OLD TRUCK

 Norton Young Readers • An Imprint of W. W. Norton and Company

On a small farm, an old truck worked hard.

The old truck worked long.

The old truck grew weary and tired.

So the old truck rested

and dreamed.

The old truck sailed the seas,

braved the skies,

and chased the stars.

But the old truck grew older.

And older.

And older still.

On a small farm, a new farmer worked hard.

The new farmer worked long.

The new farmer grew weary and tired.

But she dreamed

and persisted.

VROOOOOOOM!!

On a small farm, an old truck worked hard.